BAP Publication Presents

New Year 2023

Compiled by

Nikhil Jain

COPYRIGHT

Copyright © 2022 **New Year 2023**

Copyright © 2022 Nikhil Jain

Editor – Nikhil Jain
Illustrator – Nikhil Jain
Cover Designer – Nikhil Jain

MRP: 149/-

Published by BAP Publication
Mumbai

This book has been published with all reasonable efforts taken to make the material error-free after the consent of all the co-authors. Co-authors of this book are solely responsible and liable or its content including but not limited to the views, representations, descriptions, statements, information, opinions, and references.

The Publisher and Editor shall not be liable whatsoever for any errors, omissions, whether such omissions result from negligence, accident, or any other cause or claims for loss or damages of any kind, including without limitation, indirect or consequential loss or damage arising out of use, inability to use, or about the reliability, accuracy or sufficiency of the information contained in this book.

DISCLAIMER

This is a pure work of fiction. Unless otherwise indicated, all the names, characters, businesses, places, events and incidents in this book are either the product of the author's imagination or used in a fictitious manner. Any resemblance to actual persons, living or dead, or actual events is purely coincidental.

ACKNOWLEDGEMENT

The completion of this anthology would not have been possible without the kind cooperation of all the amazing writers from all over India. We thank everyone whole heartedly who all have worked so hard for this book and have contributed their valuable time and efforts to make this anthology a huge success.

DESCRIPTION OF THE BOOK

New Year 2023 is the book that talks about the imagination of different Co-authors. Every individual has penned their own expression and thoughts. This is all about penning down the words of different person based on their imaginations and sometimes on life experiences. We just shared our muses through scribbling it in our own way. This book isn't to harm anyone's experiences or thoughts of any individual. Anything in this book is not merely to offend anyone's thought.

INDEX

Founder

Compiler

Co-Authors

ABOUT THE FOUNDER
PATHAN FATIMA

Pathan Fatima,CEO of Bap Publication .She helps the people to publish their talent in different anthologies and solo book for free for the one who can't afford the price of publishing . She love to write poem's , stories , quotes , in format of fictional and non fictional both . She is hailing from Mumbai. Also she is co-author in many famous anthologies .Also she is a author in the book name as "Pilot with ink" , Basically she is all rounder interested in every curriculum activities . she is looking towards her dream and working hard to make it true . currently she is pursuing Aircraft maintenance engineering plus Bsc in aeronautics also she aims to be a future pilot . She started her journey as a writer long back ago, most of her poems will inspire you to bring the best in you. Though the write ups are small, the meaning will be deeper and penned directly from her heart . She is a kind of a person who will become your friend and bring a smile on your face also she will help you whenever you will need her .

Instagram: Captain_emaaaa

Bap_publication

Mail me at : fatimapathan156@gmail.com

THE NEW

And so it begins How have I already fallen behind I do not feel refreshed, I have not been restored, I did not hit the ground running but rolled from my sheets this colorless morning my eyes battling a foe that told them to stay down my head tumbling from one fog into another upon recalling that what was still is, that December conjures no magic in its reappearance as January

So today I will open a window, feel the bracing air like a fighter who gets her second wind I'll linger and play with my dog until his tongue rolls long and low I'll build the border of a puzzle, stand from my desk before the sun starts its setting, remove backpacks from tired shoulders, plant kisses on cold cheeks and call it a day lived.

THE END

It's done now,

The curtains will close.

We're still here, Against odds we cannot even begin to fathom.

There is beauty in the endings, Especially when we are gifted with

A new beginning, just seconds later.

So here's to us.

Here's to you.

And if you're lucky enough to be with someone That you love, and

who loves you, When the clock strikes 12 tonight,

Count your lucky stars.

Count them hard.

And for the ones who cannot be with us,

Let us imagine them here.

Fully imagine them,

With love.

COMPILER
NIKHIL JAIN

निखिल जैन, पेशे से व्यापारी, शौक से लेखक धुले, महाराष्ट्र से संबंध रखते हैं। इन्हें शैक्षिक तौर पर BBM एवं MBA की degree प्राप्त है। इन्हें अपना ज्ञान दूसरो के साथ साझा करना, यात्राएँ करना, नई नई खोज करना और रचनात्मकता से अपनी प्रतिभाओं को बेहतर बनाना अत्यंत प्रिय है। इन्हें लिखना पसंद है, क्योंकि इनका मानना है, कि लेखन से हम अपनी आंतरिक भावनाओं का भली भांति बखान कर सकते हैं, क्योंकि जो कहा नहीं जा सकता

उसे लिखकर व्यक्त करने में आसानी होती है और व्यक्ति का हृदय और मस्तिष्क दोनों को प्रभावित किया जा सकता है।

बतौर लेखक अपनी यात्रा का प्रारंभ करने वाले निखिल ने लेखन जगत में हो रही राजनीति के दुष्प्रभावों को नजरंदाज ना करते हुए नव लेखकों के हित में कार्य करने हेतु कुछ प्रयास करने का सोचा और इसी सोच के चलते नव लेखकों की प्रतिभाओं को एक मंच प्रदान करने के लिए स्वयं का प्रकाशन स्थापित किया और इसी दौर में ये अब Unité Publication और love.vibes143 के संयोजक हैं। ये स्वयं 500 से अधिक पुस्तकों में बतौर सह लेखक एवं 85 से अधिक पुस्तकों के संकलक रह चुके हैं।

Bap publication में संपादक प्रबंधन की भूमिका निभाने वाले निखिल जैन एम एस केशरी पब्लिकेशन के सह संस्थापक के रूप में कार्यभार बखूबी संभाल रहे हैं।

हाल ही में निखिल जैन के नाम Inkzoid books of records के तहत काफ़ी विश्व रिकॉर्ड्स दर्ज किये गए हैं, जिनमें से एक "100 sainos" (First book entirely based on saino, written by 6 different writers from 6 different cities)", एक "गागर में सागर" (Which consists more than 10 different styles, composed in 7 different native and foreign languages) नामक पुस्तक के नाम दर्ज हैं जो स्वयं में

अनूठी पुस्तकें हैं। हाल ही में निखिल जी ने मुंबई इंडियंस के ऊपर एक अक्षरबद्ध कविताओं की किताब लिखी हैं, और वो किताब भी Inkzoid books of records और Glorious Book of World Records 2022 में दर्ज किये हैं।

Lovers.stop_143 नामक एक ई_पेज के सहायक प्रबंधन के तौर पर भूमिका निभाने वाले निखिल सदैव प्रयासरत रहते हैं, कि नव युवाओं को एक मंच प्रदान किया जा सके। अभी कुछ दिन पहले उन्हें The Top 22 Sensational Writers of India स्थान दिया गया है। 2021 वर्ष में इन्हे The Opus Talent Awardees से सन्मानित किया गया, यह न्यूज Fab World Today, Time Bulletin पर उपलब्ध है। इनसे जुड़ने के लिए आप संपर्क कर सकते हैं -

इंस्टाग्राम :- @love.vibes143

ईमेल :- love.vibes143@outlook.com

संकल्प

कुछ नया किया है, कुछ पुराने को साथ लेकर, क्योंकि भूत से सबक लेकर भविष्य की योजना बनाई जाएं, तो एक बेहतर वर्तमान की नींव रखी जा सकती है।

व्यक्तित्व में बदलाव आसान नहीं, तो कोई भी ऐसा संकल्प, जो हमारी महत्वकांक्षाओं को ठेस पहुँचायें, सही मायनों में उचित तो नहीं है, इसलिए संकल्प करेंगे अपनी गलतिया सुधार, उन्हें फिर से ना दोहराने का, सभी को साथ लेकर आगे बढ़ने का, एक बेहतर भविष्य निर्माण का, सभी के साथ स्वयं के भी हित में सोचने का, इस नववर्ष संकल्प लेते हैं, समाज की जगह सोच बदलने का, एक नई शुरुआत खुद से करने का।।

CO-AUTHORS

URMI YASH

Urmi Yash is a native of Nainital, currently she resides in Delhi. She is a writer as well as a teacher. She has done M.A.(English, Education) and B.A. Ed.(English) studies. Recently, she has contributed as a co-author in some compilations. She loves to write poems, articles, and stories. Her writings always reveal her feelings. Instagram handle:@mystery-of-my-words

NEW YEAR

New Year is one event that everyone is highly excited about for several reasons. New Year stirs new hopes and expectations about life around us. Every New Year reminds us of the progress in our lives. We eagerly look for some change and betterment with the arrival of every New Year. In this regard, New Year is a symbol of hope, faith, confidence and growth.On this New Year, may you change your direction and not dates, change your commitments and not the calendar, change your attitude and not the actions, and bring about a change in your faith, your force, AND your focus and not the fruit. May you live up to the promises you have made and may you create for you and your loved ones the happiest New Year ever.A new year is like starting a new chapter in your life. It's your chance to write an incredible story for yourself. May this coming year lead you on a new exciting adventure, complete with life-changing experiences and deeper friendships.

PRIYANSHI KASHYAP

Priyanshi kashyap is a 16 year old girl. Living in roorkee (uttarakhand). She wants become a successful business women. She is also a co-author of more than 6 anthologies. Red belt in taekwondo. She is topper and studious in her studies as well.

"LET'S MAKE THIS YEAR MAGICAL"

A girl, who always wants to fly high, wants to achieve her goals,
and giving efforts to achieve them.

A girl, who always tries to be independent.

A girl, who always understands others.

A girl, who is very kind.

A girl, who is a little introvert.

A girl, who is always and always pure.

A girl, who never wants to live like a queen !

A girl, who is enough for herself.

A girl, who is always trying to make her parents proud.

A girl, who wants to be a topper in 10th standard.

A girl, who will definitely make her parents proud by her hard
work and she will definitely rock her board examination.

A girl, who promise herself that she will be a topper this year.

New Year 2023

A girl, who promise that she will change herself this year, and become the best version of herself.

A girl, you won't find anywhere else.

This year promise yourself to become the best version of yourself..

Happy new year to all ...

DR. SHWETA SINGH

ये कॉलेज में पढ़ाती हैं। कार्यक्रम में संचालन का कार्य भी करते है। साथ साथ लिखने का भी शौक रखते है। ये 18 साल से लिख रहे है। इनके लेख अखबार और मैगज़ीन में भी आते हैं। 400 के करीब अंथलॉजी में भाग ले चुके है। ये बस मन की भावनाएं होती हैं जो खुद ही कलम इनकी उठजाती हैं और लिख देते हैं। कभी भी दूसरों को देखकर मत लिखो या किसी प्रतियोगिता के लिए ना लिखे।

इनके लेख आप Writco, Blogger, Twitter, Wordpress, Yourquote, Dailyhunt, Instagram, Telegram, Youtube, Facebook+Page, Muuzzer, Kmuniti, Nojoto, Koo इन सभी app में Dr.Shweta Singh के नाम से article पढ़ सकते है। इनके चैनल का नाम "Dr.Shweta Singh Motivational Speaker" है। इसमें ये मोटिवेशनल लेख डालती हैं। इनकी किताब भी प्रकाशित हुई है जिनका नाम है:- मेरे सपनों की उड़ान, प्रेरणा हारना मना है, अंतर्मन की आवाज, मैं हार जाऊ ये हो नहीं सकता, मैं नारी हूं बिकाऊ नहीं। Instagram id:- @dr.Shweta_Singh

नया साल 2023

(आप सबके घर खुशियों की लहर)

हे मेरे मालिक वर्ष के समाप्त होते होते मेरे शब्दों से या मेरे कर्मो से अगर किसी को भी ठेस पहुंची हो तो मैं सच्चे हृदय से क्षमा मांगती हूं। बस एक गुजारिश है कि मेरे लफ्जों से किसी का कभी दिल ना दु:खे मेरे लफ्जों से किसी के होंसले में जान भरने की ताकत देना। किसी की टूटी उम्मीदों को फिर से जिंदा करने का होंसला देना। मेरे रब मेरे लफ्जों में इतनी जान भरना की जब कोई अपने लक्ष्य से भटक जाए तो उसे उसकी मंजिल तक पहुंचाने में सफल हो सकूं। मेरी दुआ में इतना असर देना की, मैं आपके बनाए हुए लोगों के लिए दुआ करूं और सबके घरों में खुशियां ही खुशियां महक उठें। किसी के घर के आंगन में मायूसी ना छाए। इतनी कृपया कर दीजिए मेरे मालिक कि इस साल सबकी जिंदगी में खुशियों का कहर टूट कर आए। ये साल 2023 आप सबके लिए एक यादगार पल बन जाए खुशियों की गूंज से।

SHABANA FIRDAUS

She is a teacher. Teach biology. Writing and teaching are her passion. She has written as Co-author many anthologies. She has also written a novel My Shadow and solo books petals of roses in my garden She wants to heal and enter all hearts. She believes writing is the best way to flow out all emotions in words.

NEW YEAR 2023

The new year 2023 is
On the way
Coming to us
With new hopes,
New beginning
And a new start of life.

Let this new year
Took away All the pain
Of the year 2022
That is going to depart
The new Ray's of hope
Setting out all we suffered

A new sun is going to rise
Bring joy and happiness
Let the coming year
Remove all darkness
From our life
Heal out all pains.

The success of all
Fall on their feet
All sorrows and failures
Are Dusked out
Let the depart year
Took away All odds.

YAMINI SUDARGURU

Yamini Sudarguru is a fascinating writer and poet. Her enthusiasm towards literature is always incredible. She secured many awards for poems in her school days. This made her prompt a lot in writing. Her exposure will be open for many challenges,tasks and exchange of ideas. She always wants to be surrounded with books. She published her optimistic book entitled "DONE BOOSTED UP" to motivate young conquerors and young writers. She has also been a podcaster on Spotify on the topic of "Conqueror of 2023".

NEW YEAR

The rill of life tiring us - when
The will of the heart' cuddles,
Forwarding the days furiously - Let's
Pause the cherished moments alone .

Deeper thoughts had driven me here,
Pen down my fears and tears
At the end of the year,
Providing the vibes to put me on fire.

I hope the days are better,
Thought and thinking killing me to pursue myself in a manner,
What else is the universe going to do !
Alone, all alone in the running race.

Finding my voice of consciousness,
Searching my inner peace in the year,
Floating in the boat of happiness,
Chasing the dream in the new year.

SUNITA NALWAYA

सुनीता नलवाया (मेहता) राजस्थान के सिरोही जिले में सरकारी अध्यापिका के रूप में कार्यरत है। इनकी पत्रिका में कविता छपती रहती है। इन्हे ब्लाक व जिला स्तर पर सम्मानित किया गया है। स्थानीय स्तर पर नाट्य लेखन व रूपान्तरण कहानी लेखन में भी इन्हे सम्मानित किया गया है। सहलेखिका के रूप में इन्होने कई पुस्तकों मे अपना योगदान दिया है। ऑनलाइन लेखन में भी इन्हे सम्मान मिला है।

नया साल

मुट्ठी में रेत सा समय

फिसलता रहता है

हरपल, हर घड़ी

गुजरते जाते है

उम्र के पड़ाव सालों साल

खड़े ही रह जाते हम

वही के वही साल दर साल

नए साल के इंतजार में

नया साल ले जाता है

जाने कितने अरमान

दे जाता है अनेकों सपने

कभी ना पूरे होने के लिए

फिर हम लड़ने लग जाते है

जीवन के झंझावातों से

खुशी ग़म की तलाश में

इसी में फिर आ जाता है

नया साल, हम वही पुराने।।

SUHANI PANDEY

सुहानी पाण्डे रुद्रपुर (उत्तर प्रदेश) की रहने वाली हैं। इनको लेखन में बहुत रुचि है। भक्ति, प्रेम तथा प्रेरणा पर आधारित लेखन में इन्हें बहुत रुचि है। यह अग्रेंजी तथा हिन्दी दोनों भाषाओं में लेखन का कार्य कर लेती हैं। शायरी लेखन में भी इनकी बहुत रुचि है। लिखने की प्रेरणा इसे अपने शिक्षक (अमन विवेक त्रिपाठी) तथा अपनी बहन (ऐश्वर्या त्रिपाठी) से मिली है।

नव वर्ष

वह सपना था तो टूट गया,

यह साल भी अब तो दूर गया,

है बची ख्वाब की यादें बस,

वह समय ही था जो छूट गया।

आएगा अब नया वर्ष एक,

लेके रिश्ते संघर्ष अनेक।

लोग कुछ रूठे हैं ये मान लो तुम,

दुनिया की असलियत जान लो तुम।

अब यह वर्ष गया,

सिखा के सीख नई।

किए हमने इस वर्ष भूल कई।

अब दूसरी गलती ना करना तुम

जो नया वर्ष है उसको आने दो पर पिछले से नहीं मुकरना तुम।।

NILOFAR FAROOQUI TAUSEEF

नीलोफर फारूकी तौसीफ, बिहारशरीफ, नालंदा के रहने वाली हैं लेकिन मुंबई में रहती हैं। इन्होंने एम०सी०ए० और एम०बी०ए० किया है। पेशे से आई० टी० में टीम लीडर और जुनून से लेखक हैं। अपने विचारों, भावनाओं को अपने लेखन में लिखना पसंद करती हैं। इनके लिए "कलम क्रांति लाने की तलवार है"। इनके लेख और शोध पत्र 400 से अधिक पुस्तकों और पत्रिकाओं में और देश की प्रतिष्ठित पत्रिकाओं में भी प्रकाशित हो चुके हैं। आप इनके fb और instagram को देख सकते हैं -@writernilofar

नव वर्ष अभिनन्दन

उड़ते हुए परिंदों की नई उड़ान है,
नए रंगों से रंगा ये अपना जहान है।
नए लक्ष्य लिए क़दम बढाते जाएँगे,
नए वर्ष में नई कृतिमान ही पहचान है।

प्रेम की बगिया से सजेगा ये आँगन,
मैला न होगा किसी नारी का दामन,
मन को स्वच्छता की ओर ले जायेंगे,
आओ करे सब नव वर्ष का अभिनन्दन।

नए सुर, नई आवाज़ , नई स्याही का रंग,
इंद्रधनुष के भाँति, सतरंगा हो उमंग,
हर ज़ुल्म के ख़िलाफ़ आवाज़ उठाएंगे,
मुहब्बत की हार तार में होगी नई तरंग।

नई उम्मीद का दीया दिल में जलाएँ,
टूटे हुए ख़्वाब को नए पंख दे आएँ,
मानवता ही नई मिसाल है मानव की,
दुनिया को नव वर्ष में पाठ पढ़ाएँ।

हर्षोल्लास से सबका मन तृप्त रहे,
दिल और देश पे कृपा बनी रहे,
शिक्षा के उज्यारा से तारों की चमक हो,
नव वर्ष में नई किरण सजी रहे।।

PRIYANSHU CHOUDHARY

प्रियांशु चौधरी,यह वर्तमान समय में अभी छात्राध्यापक है और बालाघाट जिले के तहसील कटंगी के shivam college katangi से d el ed कर रहे हैं। प्रियांशु चौधरी को बचपन से बहुत सी एक्टिविटीज में भाग लेना अच्छा लगता था जैसे गीत ,भाषण ,डांस, नाटक और शेर ,शायरी लिखना और कविता बनाना।

धीरे धीरे इन्हे कविता लिखने का शौक ऐसा हुआ की इन्होंने सन 2018 से खुद की कहानी , कविता लिखना शुरू कर दी और लिखते लिखते इन्हे पूरे 5 साल हो गए।

प्रियांशु चौधरी का बचपन महकेपार गांव में बीता जो बालाघाट जिले के तहसील तिरोड़ी में आता है और इसी महकेपार गांव के स्कूल से अपनी प्रारंभिक शिक्षा पूर्ण की ।

अब आगे की शिक्षा भी यह प्राप्त करना चाहते थे जिसके लिए इन्होंने बहुत से कॉलेज में अप्लाई किया लेकिन इनका नाम pg College balaghat की bsc pcm की मेरिट लिस्ट में आया और इन्होने pg College balaghat से सन 2018 से 2021 में अपना gradution यानि bsc पूर्ण किया।

Pcm का तात्पर्य यह था की physics, chemistry, mathmatics जो की bsc में इनके विषय थे।

नया साल 2023

स्वागत है स्वागत है,नए वर्ष का तहे दिल से स्वागत है।

अभिनंदन है अभिनंदन है, नए वर्ष में आप सभी का अभिनंदन है।

आ रहा है नया वर्ष एक नई शुरुवात लेकर,अपनो के बीच एक
नया माहौल लेकर।

जा रहा है यह वर्ष न जानी कितनी यादों को लेकर

शुक्रगुजार हैं शुक्रगुजार हैं यह वर्ष तेरा शुक्रगुजार हैं।

स्वागत है...

नए वर्ष में एक ही कामना सबसे करते है ,सबके मन में रहे प्यार

हमारी खातिर यही आस बनाए रखते हैं।

यह नए वर्ष तेरा स्वागत हम करते हैं।

हस रहे हैं तो कोई चमक रहे हैं तेरे आने पर, लोगो के मन में
खुशियां आ गई है तेरे आने पर

तेरे साथ में होने से ऐसी ही खुशियां रहे ऐसी कामना सभी से
करते हैं।

यह नए वर्ष तेरा स्वागत हम तहे दिल से करते हैं।

स्वागत है...

कुछ ख्वाब देखे हैं हमने जो तेरे आने पर पूरे होंगे, हमारे पराए
भी जल्द अपने होंगे
जिनके मन में रहती थी कठुरता हमारी खातिर अब उनके मन में
प्यार भी आयेगा जब तेरा साथ मिलता रहेगा।
स्वागत है... स्वागत है...

RAMNEHA PANDEY

रामनेहा पाण्डे लखनऊ (उत्तर प्रदेश) से हैं। लिखना इनके विचारों को आगे बढाता हैं। रामनेहा जी को लिखना काफी पसन्द हैं। अपने विचारों से समाज में फैली कुरितियां को समाप्त कर ऊंच-नीच के भेदभाव और जड़ से खत्म करना चाहती हैं। एक समाज सेविका बनकर अनाथ और गरीब बच्चों की शिक्षा पर काम करना चाहती हैं।

नई उड़ान

मन चचंल हैं तन पुलकित हैं नये वर्ष के आने से,
हर्षित हैं जग सारा कुछ नया कर जाने से।

रूठो को मना लो प्रेम की नदियां बहा दो,
नया दिन नई उमगें नई किरण वेला में
सर्वस्य नया बना दो।

उठो जागो कर्मभूमि के पथ पर खुद को समर्पित कर डालो,
हुई हैं पुलिकित अश्रु -धारा, अव मन के मैल धुल डालो।

नये दिन की नई किरण में नया कुछ कर डालो,
अब हृदय पवित्र हुआ ही हैं तो सत् मार्ग पर लगा डालो।

हर्षित हैं आज प्रकृति भी कि कुछ तो मानव बदला हैं,
देखो आज उसने अपने मन में प्रेम, उत्साह का दीप जलाया हैं।

नये दिन की नई वेला में नया तुम कर डालो,
कोई दुखी और भूखा न सो पाये इस पृथ्वी पर ऐसा प्रण कर डालो।।

SONAL LUDARIYA

Sonal Ludariya is an postgraduate and CA Final Student.She is also a passionate writer who fills her poetry with immense courage and a new perspective of youth and their new challenges that connects her more to the audience who loves to read and wants to see a change in society.

आशा

निराशा जब अपनी चरम सीमा पर हो,

हर एक दिन जसे खुद पर ही बोझ हो,

तुम उदासी का दरिया पार कर चुके हो,

अब उसके बाद वाला सुखा तुम्हारा जीवन हो।

दिल चीख रहा हो पर लबों के पास शब्द ना हो,

सांसे तो चल रही है पर तुम अपने सपनों को मार चुके हो,

सब कुछ हो पर सुनेपन में डूबा हुआ,

गुहार लगाने पर भी जब ना सुनवाई हो।

ऐसे में तुम जब एक पहला दिया आशा का नए साल में जलाओगे,

अपनी जितनी शेष सारी शक्तियाँ और पिछले साल के दर्दो की लौं बनोगे,

अंधेरा सारा मन का मिट जाएगा और जहां था सुखा वही तुम्हारी

खुशियों के फूल होंगे,

जो तुमने लगाये थे उसके ही फल होंगे,

जानती हूँ नहीं होगा आसान फिर भी तुम अपना तिनका ढूंढ़ लाओगे,

उस पर होकर सवार तुम एक नयी क्रान्ति का आरम्भ करोगे।।

MAYURI THAKRE

मयूरी ठाकरे बालाघाट जिले के तहसील कटंगी के छोटे से गांव पाथरवाड़ा में रहती है। मयूरी ठाकरे अभी वर्तमान समय में अतिथि शिक्षक है और इन्हे लेखक कला में रुचि है।

नया साल

नया नया सा ये जहां

नई नई सी ख्वाहिश है

नया नया हैं आसमान   ये

तेरे आने की आहट है

जिंदगी है छोटी सी और मुस्कुराना बाकी हैं

नया नया सा ये जहाँ

नई नई   सी ख्वाहिश हैं

नया साल नई ख्वाहिशे

नई उमंगे सिखाती है

बिखरती है सारी खुशियां

खुशहाली राग सुनाती है

लगे है नित नैन हमारे तेरे

आने पर शुभ आगमन हो तेरा

यही याद दिलाती हैं

बिखरती है सारी खुशियां खुशहाली राग   सुनातीं हैं

AALIYAH STARK

She is born and brought up in Kerala. She is a teacher who is also pursuing her post-graduation in English. Her greatest dream and passion is to become a published author, and she is slowly taking those small steps towards the heights she has set. Aaliyah is a published author and a webnovel writer. She has also been part of numerous anthologies under various publications writing poems, articles, and short stories using her pseudonym Aaliyah Stark. Currently, she is working with BeTales Magazine, India's first-ever teenage magazine, as their episodic and content writer.

LOST AND FOUND

Lost focus, lost in the woods,

Lost the way, Lost in the darkness,

Lost the mind, Lost the heart,

Lost a life, that could have become the best,

Somewhere that's less travelled, less touched,

Somewhere buried into the unknown depths.

Don't want to be drowned,

But neither to be found.

To all those lies, and fake declaration of love.

Yet I found courage, to leave the past behind,

As the New Year fast approached me,

Giving a chance write again in the blank slate.

About my future, my life changing choices,

Not the one that made me fall but one that would take me to the sky.

BITTHEL AGARWALA

The writer is born and brought up in Malda, West Bengal, completed std.10 from North Point English Academy, Malda, completed std.XII from Delhi Public School, Megacity. Currently persuing BBA from SMIT,Sikkim. Writing, singing, creativity and Art is major interest field. He loves to learn about different cultures, travel and family. Looking forward to grow and develop along with the rural sector of society and bring out the hidden stories for the world.

NEW YEAR 2023

New Year is not only to celebrate,
It is realization to understand the mistakes of life,
The lesson which we get from past year is the actual life-long
lesson,
The upcoming year is to upgrade ourselves.

Every year we celebrate the welcome of the year,
Girls don't wear winter clothes in order to show,
Boys wear full clothes as they feel more cold than girls,
Both are same as ice of the same nature.

Time is changing but the world is still the same,
The thoughts of human beings have changed,
The celebration of New Year should be with food, fun, masti with
family and friends,
It is a common saying if the end is good starting is good.

SURAPRATAP KAMILA

Surapratap kamila is a self motivated and conscientious youth, son of Mr. Gourahari Kamila & Mrs. Sandhyarani Kamila, hailing from the beautiful city of Balasore, Odisha. He has done his master's in English from Berhampur University, Odisha, and presently he is pursuing his Integrated BED MED degree in Central University of Kashmir. He has faced numerous tassel to reach his destiny as he has some financial problems . But he never allow these circumstances to let him down and the challenges keeps motivating him moving towards his goal, passion and life. He adores nature so he take nature for the subject of his writings. "The Road not taken" by Robert Frost and "Oh Captain My Captain" by Walt Whitman and also many other poems inspired him to write something. His passion to write and to study English literature gives a fuel to his life. He wants to became a professor. He has written some love poems, his fantasy to write something visionary poem and a very enthusiastic idea to write about 21st century people's life and their thoughts.

THIS NEW YEAR

This new year,
Hope, for a better future,
Hope, for a new adventure,
In a new year that comes
To be filled with memories and fun.

This new year,
Hope, for some justice,
Hope, for some service
To be rightfully served,
Specifically provided
For those mistreated.

This new year,
Hope, for progress,
Hope, for success.
Set high is the bar
To achieve so far,
For those with big dreams.

This new year,
Hope, for peace,
Hope, for a cease,
Stopping any violence
Or forced silence,
For those suffering.

This new year,
Hope, for the world,
And ease from the hardships hurled
Towards the population
Of every single nation.
Hope.

MEHJABIN BAIG

Mehjabin is a Student pursuing BSc. She belongs to Mumbai. Her Hobby includes Reading,singing and Calligraphy. More often than you'll find obsessing over Novels,Music along side a cup of tea.

AN ANOTHER YEAR

An another year passed,
An another year came,
An another friend left ,
Another friend entered with different name.

The previous year was full of chaos,
But honestly it was a great teacher,
It taught us a great lesson that -
That life is about "or " or "either".

Being grateful for what you have,
Being grateful for who you are,
But never be so satisfied,
Because the destination is yet,too far.

With the new resolutions,
Let's welcome the new year,
Evolving as a person,
By kicking out our fear.

Being honest to ourselves,
Making the right decision,
Open a new chapter of life,
Face it, make it and broad the vision.

MANI KUMAR POLE

Mani Kumar Pole is a C.M.A Student from Hyderabad, Telangana. The Author/Writer/Poet loves acting, dancing, sketching an art, travelling and martial arts. He pens out his emotion's and feelings through his writings. He loves storytelling and hopes to tell more and more stories which will resonate with every one's heart. The author seeks for a career in writing apart from his usual profession. "The world is never the same once a good poem is added to it".

TOME OF LIFE

Started my day with crazy thoughts in my mind.
With the great charm which I shall carry through out the day.

Surprisingly noticed a book opened on my desk,
Where pages of the book were filled with unpredictable events
And every page I read carried different kind of emotions,
Every unpleasant situation here had a reason
But those reasons ended up losing relations.

I started blubbing by reading those flaws of mine
But was causious not repeating the same blunders again.
Some of these pages include black spots
Which motivated me to fill the upcoming pages,
With all shining & glittering memories.

Its your turn to open a new page of your life
And start filling it with great & awful memories
Cuz you never know where that tome hidden its last page of life.

SYED MUNTAZEER

सैयद मुंताजीर अहमद अदिलाबाद के रहने वाले है। वह एक इंजिनियर है। सैयद शायरो के घराने से ताल्लुकात रखते है। उन्होंने दसवीं कक्षा से लिखना शुरू किया था। सैयद के गुरु उन्हें अदब के नाम से पुकारते थे और इसीलिए सैयद लेखन की दुनिया में अदब मुंताजीर बनकर कर कदम रखा। अदब को इस दुनिया से और अपनी क्रश से लिखने की प्रेरणा मिलती है। आप उन्हें इंस्टाग्राम पर **Man_marzi_yan** से जुड़ सकते हैं और यूट्यूब में **Adab Muntazeer** पर उनकी कविताएं सुन सकते हैं।

एक खत नए साल का

TO : XXXX

प्रेषक: अदब मुंतज़ीर

माना के मुश्किल था सफर
मगर गुजर गया,
कोई मिला दौर-ए-जिंदगी में
फिर बिछड़ गया।

कोई मायूस रहा साल भर
तो कोई खुशी से मर गया,
कोई दर गया जिम्मेदारियों से
कोई जिम्मेदारियों में बिखर गया।

किसी को वफ़ा मिली किसी से
कोई बेवफा से मोहब्बत कर गया,
कोई सच्ची मोहब्बत में हार गया
तो कोई झूट बोल आगे गया।

ये सिल सिला है जिंदगी का
चलता ही जाएगा,
कोई मिलता है, बिछड़ता जाएगा
कोई पता, खोता जाएगा।

एक नई उम्मीद एक नई उमंग के साथ।
करो न्ए साल के न्ए दिन की शुरुआत।।